The Story of FERDINAND

by Munro Leaf
illustrated by Robert Lawson

Grosset & Dunlap
An Imprint of Penguin Group (USA) Inc.

GROSSET & DUNLAP
Published by the Penguin Group
Penguin Group (USA) Inc., 375 Hudson Street, New York, New York 10014, USA
Penguin Group (Canada), 90 Eglinton Avenue East, Suite 700, Toronto, Ontario M4P 2Y3, Canada
(a division of Pearson Penguin Canada Inc.)
Penguin Books Ltd., 80 Strand, London WC2R 0RL, England
Penguin Group Ireland, 25 St. Stephen's Green, Dublin 2, Ireland
(a division of Penguin Books Ltd.)
Penguin Group (Australia), 250 Camberwell Road, Camberwell, Victoria 3124, Australia
(a division of Pearson Australia Group Pty. Ltd.)
Penguin Books India Pvt. Ltd., 11 Community Centre,
Panchsheel Park, New Delhi—110 017, India
Penguin Group (NZ), 67 Apollo Drive, Rosedale, North Shore 0632, New Zealand
(a division of Pearson New Zealand Ltd.)
Penguin Books (South Africa) (Pty.) Ltd., 24 Sturdee Avenue,
Rosebank, Johannesburg 2196, South Africa

Penguin Books Ltd., Registered Offices: 80 Strand, London WC2R 0RL, England

First published by The Viking Press 1936

The Library of Congress has cataloged the previous Grosset & Dunlap edition under the following Control Number: 00-057791

ISBN 978-0-448-45694-2   20 19 18 17 16 15

Once upon a time in Spain

there was a little bull and
his name was Ferdinand.

All the other little bulls
he lived with would run and jump
and butt their heads together,

but not Ferdinand.

He liked to sit just quietly and
smell the flowers.
He had a favorite spot out in
the pasture under a cork tree.
It was his favorite tree and he
would sit in its shade all day
and smell the flowers.

Sometimes his mother,
who was a cow,
would worry about him.
She was afraid he would
be lonesome all by himself.

"Why don't you run and play with the other little bulls and skip and butt your head?" she would say. But Ferdinand would shake his head. "I like it better here where I can sit just quietly and smell the flowers."

His mother saw that he was not lonesome, and because she was an understanding mother, even though she was a cow, she let him just sit there and be happy.

As the years went by
Ferdinand grew and
grew until he was
very big and strong.

FERDINAND
2years

FERDINAND
1year

3 MONTHS

1 week

RL

All the other bulls who had grown
up with him in the same pasture
would fight each other all day.
They would butt each other and
stick each other with their horns.
What they wanted most of all was
to be picked to fight at the bull
fights in Madrid.

But not Ferdinand—
he still liked to sit just
quietly under the cork tree
and smell the flowers.

One day five men came in very funny hats to pick the biggest, fastest, roughest bull to fight in the bull fights in Madrid.

All the other bulls ran around snorting and butting, leaping and jumping so the men would think that they were very very strong and fierce and pick them.

Ferdinand knew that
they wouldn't pick him
and he didn't care. So
he went out to his favorite
cork tree to sit down.

RL

He didn't look where he was sitting and instead of sitting on the nice cool grass in the shade he sat on a bumble bee.

Well, if you were a bumble bee and a bull sat on you what would you do? You would sting him. And that is just what this bee did to Ferdinand.

Wow! Did it hurt! Ferdinand
jumped up with a snort. He
ran around puffing and snorting,
butting and pawing the
ground as if he were crazy.

RL

The five men saw him and they
all shouted with joy. Here was
the largest and fiercest bull of
all. Just the one for the bull
fights in Madrid!

So they took him
away for the
bull fight day
in a cart.

What a day it was! Flags were flying, bands were playing . . . and all the lovely ladies had flowers in their hair.

They had a parade into the bull ring.

First came the Banderilleros
with long sharp pins with
ribbons on them to stick in the
bull and make him mad.

Next came the Picadores who rode skinny horses and they had long spears to stick in the bull and make him madder.

Then came the Matador, the proudest of all—he thought he was very handsome, and bowed to the ladies. He had a red cape and a sword and was supposed to stick the bull last of all.

Then came the bull, and you
know who that was don't you?
—FERDINAND.

They called him Ferdinand the Fierce and all the Banderilleros were afraid of him and the Picadores were afraid of him and the Matador was scared stiff.

Ferdinand ran to
the middle of the
ring and everyone
shouted and clapped
because they thought
he was going to fight
fiercely and butt
and snort and stick
his horns around.

But not Ferdinand. When he
got to the middle of the ring
he saw the flowers in all the
lovely ladies' hair and he just
sat down quietly and smelled.

He wouldn't fight and be fierce no matter what they did. He just sat and smelled. And the Banderilleros were mad and the Picadores were madder and the Matador was so mad he cried because he couldn't show off with his cape and sword.

So they had to take Ferdinand home.

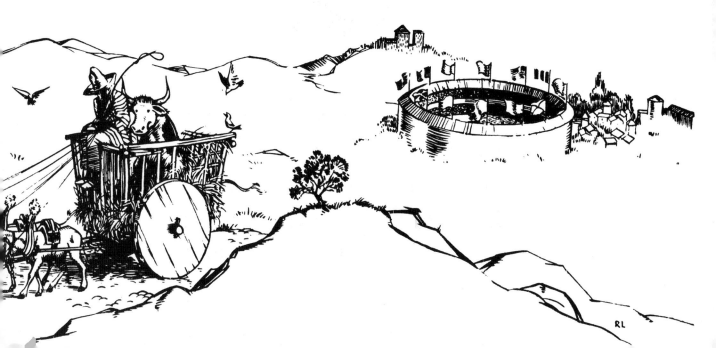

And for all I know he is sitting there still, under his favorite cork tree, smelling the flowers just quietly.

He is very happy.